KATHI APPELT

Merry Christmas, Merry Crow

ILLUSTRATED BY

JON GOODELL

HARCOURT, INC. ◆ Orlando Austin New York San Diego Toronto London

Requests for permission to make copies of any
part of the work should be mailed to the following
address: Permissions Department, Harcourt, Inc.,
6277 Sea Harbor Drive, Orlando, Florida
32887-6777.

www.HarcourtBooks.com

Library of Congress Cataloging-in-Publication Data
Appelt, Kathi, 1954–
Merry Christmas, merry crow/Kathi Appelt;
illustrated by Jon Goodell.
p.   cm.
Summary: A busy crow flies around town picking
up all kinds of discarded items and uses them to
create a beautiful Christmas tree.
[1. Crows—Fiction. 2. Christmas trees—Fiction.
3. Stories in rhyme.]
I. Goodell, Jon, ill.   II. Title.
PZ8.3.A554Me   2005
[E]—dc21   2002012641
ISBN 0-15-202651-7

First edition
H G F E D C B A

Printed in Singapore

The illustrations in this book were painted in oil
and acrylic on canvas.
The display type was set in Truesdell Italic and
Opti Dianna Script.
The text type was set in Truesdell.
Color separations by Bright Arts ltd., Hong Kong
Printed and bound by Tien Wah Press, Singapore
This book was printed on totally chlorine-free
Stora Enso Matte paper.
Production supervision by Pascha Gerlinger
Designed by Linda Lockowitz

For Heather Nicole McKay and Kaliska Carey Ross, treasures!

—K. A.

For Kathi, with thanks for the gift of her wonderful words

—J. G.

Wind's a blowin'
Sky's a snowin'
Where's this feathered
fellow goin'?

Round the chimneys
Over the yards
Down the busy boulevards

A button here
A feather there
　　A crow can find things anywhere!

A strand of tinsel
　Twigs and twine
　　Berries from a twisty vine

'Cross the plaza
Through the zoo
Along the crowded avenue

A shiny ring

A piece of string

A length of garland glimmering

Colored glass

A bottle cap

Fancy gold and silver wrap

Behind the market
Past the shops

This crow is making all the stops!

A broken chain

A lonely sock

A single key without its lock

Some scraps of cloth
A crimson bow
A perfect sprig
    of mistletoe

Hustle, bustle
Coming, going
So much busy
to and fro-ing

What's his hurry?
What's his mission?
What's his secret expedition?

A silky flower
A paper star
A misbegotten racing car

Candy wrappers
Red and brown
A treasure lost, a treasure found

Atop the flagpole
'Midst the seats

Up and down the snowy streets

Jangly tags
A tiny wheel
A luscious curl of orange peel

A string of beads
A tinkly bell
What's he doing? Will he tell?

One last stop
A bag of seeds

That's everything this tired crow needs

A flap of wings
A cry of glee—
  What a perfect Christmas tree!

A magic sight
All hearts aglow

Merry Christmas, merry crow!